Dear mouse friends,
Welcome to the world of

Geronimo Stilton

THE RODENT'S GAZETTE
EDITORIAL STAFF

Geronimo Stilton
A learned and brainy
mouse; editor of
The Rodent's Gazette

Thea Stilton
Geronimo's sister and
special correspondent at
The Rodent's Gazette

Trap Stilton
An awful joker;
Geronimo's cousin and
owner of the store
Cheap Junk for Less

Benjamin Stilton
A sweet and loving
nine-year-old mouse;
Geronimo's favorite
nephew

Geronimo Stilton

THE SUPER CHEF CONTEST

Scholastic Inc.

ISBN 978-9-351-03328-8

Based on an original idea by Elisabetta Dami.

www.geronimostilton.com

Published by Scholastic Inc., 557 Broadway, New York, NY 10012. SCHOLASTIC and associated logos are trademarks and/or registered trademarks of Scholastic Inc.

Stilton is the name of a famous English cheese. It is a registered trademark of the Stilton Cheese Makers' Association. For more information, go to www.stiltoncheese.com.

Text by Geronimo Stilton
Original title *La Gara dei Supercuochi*
Cover by Giuseppe Ferrario (design) and Giulia Zaffaroni (color)
Illustrations by Danilo Barozzi (design), Carolina Livio (ink), and Christian Aliprandi (color)
Graphics by Chiara Cebraro

Special thanks to AnnMarie Anderson
Translated by Andrea Schaffer
Interior design by Kay Petronio

First printing, October 2014

Reprinted by Scholastic India Pvt. Ltd., 2014 (Thrice), 2015 (Five times), 2016, 2017 (Thrice), 2018 (Thrice)

Printed in India by Repro India Ltd.

BANG, BANG, BANG . . . BANG!

It was a **BEAUTIFUL** morning. The first rays of the sun peeked through my curtains, warming the blankets on my cozy bed. I was tucked in *peacefully*, the covers pulled up, snoring like a hibernating dormouse.

Oops! I always forget to introduce myself: My name is Stilton, *Geronimo Stilton*.

I'm the editor of *The Rodent's Gazette*, the most **FAMOUSE** newspaper on Mouse Island.

Anyway, I was **dreaming** of biting into my favorite breakfast treat (a cheese-filled donut with **vanilla** frosting) when suddenly I heard a **deafening** sound outside. What was that terrible noise? It sounded more or less like this:

Bang, bang, bang . . .

BANG!!!

I jumped out of bed with a **SQUEAK**. Then I threw open the window and something wet, mushy, and **smelly** hit me right in the snout. **Splat!**

UGH! I spat out the soggy substance, which had a **STRANGE** odor. What could it be?

"Aaarrrgggh!" I squeaked. "Who's there? What was that?"

Then I heard a familiar voice: "Cousin!" the voice boomed. "Do you care about me or not?"

Only then did i understand . . .

That maybe . . .
NO, Probably. . .
NO, Surely it was . . .
my cousin, Trap Stilton!

"So, did you like it?" Trap yelled loudly.

"Wh-what was I supposed to like?" I sputtered in response. "I don't understand!"

As I was squeaking, Trap used a small wind-up catapult to shoot another SMELLY

BROWN GLOB at me. It landed right in my mouth.

I spat it out. It tasted disgusting.

"No!" I yelled. "I don't like it! But what is it?"

"It's a liver-flavored, deep-fried, CHEDDAR CHEESE meatball!" he announced proudly.

Then he began to interrogate me. "Why don't you like it? What would you CHANGE? Is it too sweet or too salty or too spicy or too bland or too dense or too soft or too —"

"Stop!" I yelled, cutting him off. "I just don't like it, and that's that. Ugh!"

But Trap just pulled a **NOTEBOOK** out of his pocket and began to write **FURIOUSLY**.

"'The victim — I mean, the taster — I mean, the assistant said he doesn't like it, and that's that. Ugh!'"

Then he snapped shut the notebook.

"You know, Geronimo, this doesn't **work** for me," he said.

"What doesn't work for you?" I asked, confused.

"These **tasting** notes!" Trap squeaked. "You must be more **precise**, more **complete**, and go into more **DETAIL**. Otherwise, how will I improve the flavor of my dishes?"

The assistant says . . .

Raw Egg Smoothie (Shells Included!)

I watched from my window as Trap *dashed* inside the enormouse, two-story white camper he had parked on my front lawn. Suddenly, he popped up through the roof of the camper and **JUMPED** toward me, flying through my open window. He landed on the floor of my bedroom. I was **flabbergasted**.

"B-but . . . the camper . . . the window . . . ," I squeaked, unable to complete a sentence. Then Trap stuffed a slice of cake into my snout.

"Wild onion cake with **cherry** cream cheese frosting," he announced proudly.

Blech! It was awful! It tasted like rancid trash!

I spat it out, disgusted.

"Here, Cuz!" Trap said, handing me a cup filled with a **murky-looking** liquid. "Wash it down with this!"

Blech! It was dreadful! It tasted like a raw egg smoothie, with the shells included.

I spat out the drink.

"This isn't going well, Geronimo," Trap said, shaking his snout. "You must give me more **constructive** feedback, understand?

Blech!

Raw egg smoothie (shells included!)

This isn't going well. . . .

Wild onion cake with cherry cream cheese frosting!

Otherwise, how will I win the **Super Chef Contest** and become the recipient of the **Great Golden Fork**?"

Then Trap reached over and **TWEAKED** my ear. **OUCH!**

"What are you **SQUEAKING** about?" I asked. Then I remembered an article I had published a few days earlier in *The Rodent's Gazette*. "Do you mean the upcoming **Super Chef Contest** in Gourmetville, which determines the best cook on Mouse Island?" I asked Trap.

GOURMETVILLE is a small town and the capital of the region of Cheese and Honey, which is famouse because it produces the best food on Mouse Island.

He reached over and tweaked my other ear. **DOUBLE OUCH!**

"**EXACTLY!**" he replied. "And do you know who will win? **Me!** But there is one little teeny, tiny detail. . . ."

He reached over and tweaked my tail. **TRIPLE OUCH!**

"I need a victim — I mean, a taster — I mean, an assistant," Trap continued. "And it's going to be **you**, Cuz!"

"B-but I can't, I really can't," I stammered. "I have so much work to do at the office. And I'm not a very good cook. Why don't you ask SOMEONE ELSE?"

Trap pointed his finger at me.

"You know, you're a really **shellfish** mouse, Geronimo," he said, poking me in

Owwwww!

You're really shellfish!

the snout. Unfortunately for me, he missed his **TARGET** and poked me in the eye instead.

"**OWWWWWW!**" I yelped with pain.

"Ha, ha, ha!" Trap laughed, **oblivious**. "Did you get my little chef pun, Cuz? *Shell*fish!

"Anyway," Trap continued, "it's got to be you. I asked Thea, but she can't because she has to accompany Aunt Sweetfur to a crochet class. I asked **coral cockle**, but she can't because she's waiting for a delivery of mussels from the Sea of Mice. I asked

I can't...

Paws Prankster

I can't...

I can't...

coral cockle

Fishyfur

my friend Paws Prankster, but he can't because he's allergic to every food except cheese and spinach. I also asked my friend Fishyfur, but he can't because he's having a birthday party for his pet fish, Red.

"I asked Tootsie from the Telltail Tavern, and he won't do it because a month ago we had a fight (in which I was right, naturally!). I even asked my friends Squeaky La Rue and Henrietta Happypaws, but they can't because . . . because . . . well, I can't remember anymore, but they can't, you see!

So now I'm asking you, Geronimo. You're my cousin, and we're **FAMILY**, right?"

He fell to his knees, pleading with me.

"I care about you, Cuz, but do you care about me?" Trap asked. "If you *do* care, you would be my assistant. If not, admit that I don't matter to you a whisker and that all you care about is your **WORK**."

Then he began to sob.

"I'm broke, G!" he squeaked. "I spent a fortune on this supercamper, which is fitted with a top-of-the-line, professional kitchen!"

"But, Trap, who made you buy an **ENORMOUSE** supercamper?" I asked.

He snorted. "Well, no one,

Huh?!

Waaaaah!

Do you care about me or not?

exactly, but . . . well, do you care about me or not?"

I sighed. It's true that I have a **heart** that's as soft as Brie cheese. I'd be willing to do almost anything for anymouse who asks for my help, even if that mouse is my IRRITATING cousin. I cleared my throat.

"Trap, if this is really that important to you, well, maybe I should . . . I would . . . well, I'll be your assistant," I agreed.

He jumped up and down with joy. Then he pulled me on board his supercamper, which was indeed fitted for a professional chef. I looked around in **shock**. There was every tool imaginable, from **A** to **Z**: from apple corers to zesters! There were the most modern appliances, a library of recipes from the most famouse chefs, and many, many other things!

1. BEDROOM, BATHROOM, AND WALK-IN CLOSET FURNISHED COMPLETELY FOR CHEFS

2. LARGE KITCHEN FITTED WITH GIANT REFRIGERATOR, FREEZER, BEVERAGE FRIDGE, APPLIANCES, POTS, PANS, AND EVERYTHING NEEDED BY THE BEST CHEFS!

3. PLACE SETTINGS FOR TWELVE, EDGED IN GOLD FOR SPECIAL OCCASIONS

4. HAND-BLOWN CRYSTAL GLASSES

5. TRAP'S MYSTERIOUS LARGE TRUNK: WHO KNEW WHAT WAS INSIDE?

6. LIBRARY OF BOOKS AND RECIPES BY THE MOST FAMOUSE CHEFS!

7. SECRET ROOM (ONLY TRAP HAD THE KEY!)

8. TELEVISION ROOM WITH VIDEO GAMES AND COMPUTER FOR RELAXATION

9. GYM TO STAY IN SHAPE

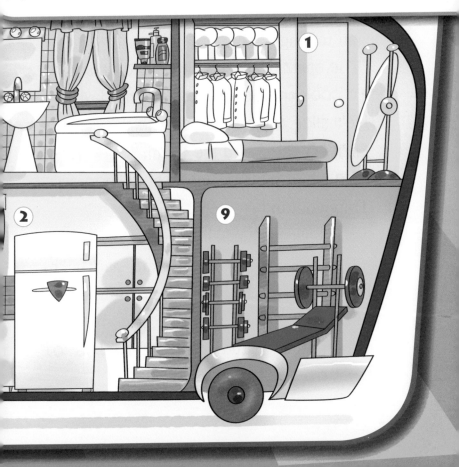

WELCOME TO
GOURMETVILLE!

Trap hopped in the driver's seat and drove off in a flash, tires **squealing**. And then he began to sing:

"The amazing Trap Stilton is on his way,
To cook the best dishes of the day!
He'll slice them and dice them,
He'll fry them and ice them,
And when he wins, we'll shout 'hooray!'"

Trap wouldn't stop chattering as we drove.

"Don't worry, Cousin," he bragged, "this contest will be a walk in the park! The **Great Golden Fork** is already mine! And do you know why? Because I'm the best! I'm prepared! I studied all the **rules of the contest**. Listen . . ."

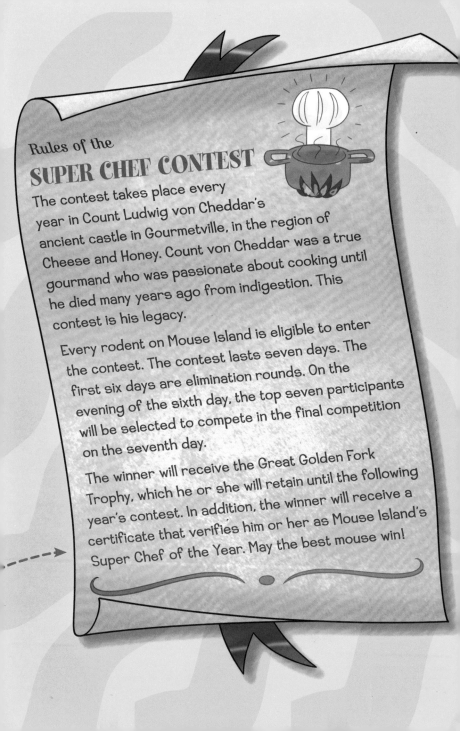

Rules of the

SUPER CHEF CONTEST

The contest takes place every year in Count Ludwig von Cheddar's ancient castle in Gourmetville, in the region of Cheese and Honey. Count von Cheddar was a true gourmand who was passionate about cooking until he died many years ago from indigestion. This contest is his legacy.

Every rodent on Mouse Island is eligible to enter the contest. The contest lasts seven days. The first six days are elimination rounds. On the evening of the sixth day, the top seven participants will be selected to compete in the final competition on the seventh day.

The winner will receive the Great Golden Fork Trophy, which he or she will retain until the following year's contest. In addition, the winner will receive a certificate that verifies him or her as Mouse Island's Super Chef of the Year. May the best mouse win!

I listened to him carefully. Moldy mozzarella! The Super Chef Contest lasted for SEVEN days. An entire week! Yikes! Poor me! This meant that I would be required to assist my cousin for SEVEN whole days ... which meant that I would have to taste yucky mush nonstop for SEVEN whole days. I became nauseated just thinking about it! Between that and the BUMPY ride in the supercamper, I was beginning to worry I might toss my cheese! Luckily, a moment later, I saw a sign that read:

MAP OF MOUSE ISLAND

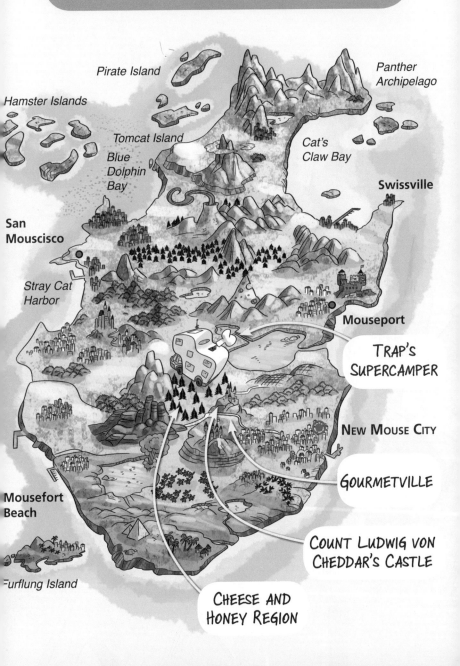

Pirate Island

Panther Archipelago

Hamster Islands

Tomcat Island

Blue Dolphin Bay

Cat's Claw Bay

Swissville

San Mouscisco

Stray Cat Harbor

Mouseport

TRAP'S SUPERCAMPER

NEW MOUSE CITY

GOURMETVILLE

COUNT LUDWIG VON CHEDDAR'S CASTLE

Mousefort Beach

Furflung Island

CHEESE AND HONEY REGION

We had arrived in Gourmetville, the capital of Mouse Island's Cheese and Honey region, which is famouse for producing the BEST food on the island. The cheeses in this city are the most delicious, the fruit is the tastiest, and the recipes are the most interesting.

I looked around: Many of Gourmetville's antique buildings were decorated with elaborate plaster like frosted birthday cakes. The streets had gourmet names: Frittata Alley, Cheesecake Lane, Sweet & Salty Street, Lasagna Way . . . the list went on and on! Street signs pointed the way to the Mouseum of Taste and the Mouseum of Cheeses.

And there were so many places to EAT! All around me there were restaurants, cafés, pizzerias, grocery stores, delis, ice cream shops, bakeries, butchers, and candy stores.

On the main street, I spotted the offices of the local **newspaper**, *The Gourmand Press*. The editors only publish recipes, results of cooking competitions, and Restaurant reviews! The streets were clogged with tourists, journalists, and chefs who had come to Gourmetville to attend the event of the year.

Trap turned down a **NARROW** street that led to a small hill in the area that surrounded the city. The supercamper climbed up the hill toward a castle perched

I'm going to win!

So many chefs!

What an event!

on the **STEEP ROCKS** overlooking Gourmetville.

It was Count von Cheddar's castle! There was a huge banner hanging over the front door:

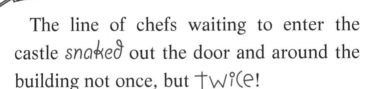

The line of chefs waiting to enter the castle *snaked* out the door and around the building not once, but twice!

FRIED SNAIL PIE
WITH OYSTER SAUCE

We got out of the **camper**, and Trap pulled out his mysterious, locked, red metal trunk. A sign on the trunk read: **Paws off!**

I wondered what was inside. Hmm! But there wasn't time to ask him about it because he was already **jostling** to get into line.

While we waited in line, I raised my **EYES** toward the castle and shivered. Dim lights shone from the highest windows, giving

No one can resist my soufflé!

We'll see who wins!

the castle a very SPOOKY
air! I remembered some
local legends I had heard —
it's said that the GHOST of
Count von Cheddar still prowls
the castle at **NIGHT**, complaining about
his indigestion.

But I didn't have time to think about it
because there were **LOTS** of journalists
hanging around the castle, and suddenly
one **recognized** me.

"Aren't you Geronimo Stilton?" he asked.
"Editor of *The Rodent's Gazette*? Are you

I'm the best chef around!

Future Super Chef here!

What a contest!

publishing a **special report** on the contest?"

"Yes, I'm Geronimo Stilton," I admitted. But before I could explain that I wasn't there as a reporter, Trap plugged my mouth with a piece of fried snail pie with oyster sauce.

"Don't get distracted!" Trap hissed as he tweaked my ear. "So, how would you rate this recipe, on a scale from one to ten?"

OUCH! And *blech*! The pie was disgusting.

"It's horrendous!" I squeaked. "I'd give it a three and a half, and that's being generous!"

But instead of being *discouraged*, Trap just continued to shove dishes into my mouth:

1 **First course:** A dark chocolate dumpling stuffed with pickles and dipped in strawberry sauce.

2 **Second course:** A goat cheese tart with a spicy orange glaze.

3 **Third course:** Beans and rice with chopped cherries and mayonnaise.

Trap pinched my other **ear**. "So?" he asked. "On a scale of one to ten, what do you think? **EIGHT**? **NINE**? Or maybe **TEN**?"

"I'd give you a negative one!" I squeaked, gagging. "All of those dishes were just **awful**!"

Trap leaned over and tweaked my **tail**.

"All right, Cuz!" he said, undeterred. "That means I'll **TRY AGAIN**! I'll make you taste many, many more dishes until they are perfect. Okay?"

I groaned. I felt **sick** to my stomach just thinking about tasting many, many more dishes! I considered ducking out of the line and trying to **escape**, but I suddenly realized that we were already in the castle and at the front of the line. A bored-looking **OFFICIAL** was questioning Trap.

"First name?" the official asked, stifling a **yawn**. "Last name? Address? Cooking experience?"

Naturally, Trap began to brag about himself: "I am Trap Stilton, the **best** cook on Mouse Island. I'm a real expert. I mean, I **UNDERSTAND** food, you know? I'm the next winner of the **Super Chef Contest**, just wait and see!"

The official snorted.

"That's what they all say," he grumbled. "If you really *are* the best, we'll all know soon enough. In the meantime, *sign* here."

He handed a sheet of paper to Trap, then assigned him a nametag in the form of a chef's hat that said: Contestant Chef Number 117.

The official interviewed me next. Then he pinned a nametag on my chest that read: Contestant Chef Number 117's Assistant. Trap grabbed a marker and crossed out Assistant and wrote Victim. Then he changed his mind and crossed it out again, writing Taster instead.

A moment later, a mouse with a megaphone made an announcement:

"Ahem!" he cleared his throat. "ATTENTION,

The Super Chef Contest
Contestant Chef Number 117's ~~Assistant~~ ~~Victim~~ Taster

contestants! Tonight you and your assistants will sleep in the rooms you have been assigned. The contest will begin tomorrow at nine a.m. sharp, in the castle's kitchen."

With a sigh, I followed Trap down a dark, dismal corridor toward the room we were assigned to share. Torches on the walls cast SUPER-SPOOKY shadows.

I shuddered with fright. Who knew if the GHOST of Count von Cheddar would

appear that night? **Yikes!**

I noted that Trap also seemed to be in a hurry to get to our room. **How strange!** He ran through the corridor, dragging the large red metal trunk behind him. **HOW VERY STRANGE!** Come to think of it, I was surprised he hadn't made **me** drag his trunk for him. **HOW VERY, VERY STRANGE!**

COBWEBS, VINTAGE CHEDDAR, AND ANCIENT STAINS!

There were two canopy beds in our room. Each bed had **red** curtains and a gold chef's hat on top. They were also covered in authentic vintage cobwebs. Dusty cooking trophies lined the mantel, and an enormouse oil painting of Count Ludwig von Cheddar hung on the wall. The painting smelled like authentic vintage mummified cheddar. And the bedspreads, curtains, tablecloths, and canopies were all stained with food: **They were authentic vintage stains!**

I looked around the room, feeling anxious. What if this had been Count von Cheddar's bedroom? My whiskers trembled as I

thought about the possibility of bumping into his ghost in the middle of the night.

Trap, on the other hand, didn't even seem to notice his surroundings. Instead, he **rushed** into the room, opened a screen in front of his bed, and pulled the red metal trunk behind it. **How strange!**

A second later, something **SHOT OUT** from behind the screen. I bent down to find that it was an electric plug. **HOW VERY STRANGE!**

An electric plug?

I stepped closer to the **screen** to give the plug back to Trap. Behind the screen, I saw my cousin reading an instruction **MANUAL**. I made out the letters *FRE* before Trap quickly moved the screen so I couldn't see anything else. How very, very strange!

"Oops, sorry!" I apologized. "I didn't mean to pry."

"Well, don't **peek** anymore!" Trap squeaked in reply. "I'm not sharing my cooking secrets with anyone, not even **YOU**, Cuz!"

Oops, sorry!

Then I heard a **CLICK**, and I immediately began to hear a strange buzzing sound that continued all night long. A few minutes later Trap began to **SNORE** loudly. *Zzzzzzz . . .*

Between the buzzing sound from behind the screen and Trap's **SNORING**, I didn't close

my eyes all **night** long.

The next morning, a loud G⊙∩G startled me. It was the signal for all of the chefs and their assistants to report to the kitchen. I dragged myself out of bed and headed straight for the MIRROR to comb my fur.

"**AHHHHH!**" I squeaked, gasping with **FRIGHT**. It was the ghost of Count von Cheddar! Trap sat up in his bed and laughed.

"Ha, ha, ha!" he **GIGGLED**. "Scared of your own reflection?"

It was true: It wasn't a ghost in the mirror — it was me! I had such **Dark Circles** under my eyes that I hadn't recognized myself. I sighed. It was going to be a **LOOOONG** week.

GERONIMO STILTON STINKS!

All of the **chefs** came out of their rooms at the same time. Trap was the only one accompanied by a victim — or rather, a taster — I mean, an assistant. Which is to say, **ME**! We all headed to the kitchen, which was a cavernous room, decorated with a collection of **antique** copper pots.

A contest official stepped forward, took an enormouse ladle, and banged it on an enormouse copper pot. **DIIINNNG!**

"The **Super Chef Contest** has begun!" he cried.

Every chef began to cook immediately. But Trap pulled out a screen from his trunk and put it in front of his stove.

"You!" he ordered me. "**VICTIM** — I mean, **TASTER** — I mean, **assistant**! Stand in front of this screen and make sure no one spies on me, got it? My recipes are **TOP SECRET**, understand?"

Then he pulled the red metal suitcase behind the **screen**, where it was out of sight.

The other chefs began to **grumble**.

"It's not fair!"

"**Contestant Chef One-seventeen** is cheating!"

My recipes are top secret!

Grrr . . .

Grrr . . .

CHARLIE CHEDDARPUFF

SAMANTHA SAVORYPAWS

An official appeared at our station, followed by a mouse pushing a cart with a giant book on top. The book was called *Rules of the Super Chef Contest*.

"All right, all right," he called out, silencing the contestants. "Let's take a look."

He pored over the rules silently for a **looong** time. Then he closed the book with a decisive **BANG**!

"There is no rule that **PROHIBITS** a

Let's take a look . . .

contestant from putting a screen in front of his or her cooking station!" he declared.

Trap peeked out from behind the screen and stuck his tongue out at everyone.

I turned bright **red** from the tip of my tail to the ends of my whiskers. Why, oh why did my cousin have to be so embarrassing?

"Ahem, excuse us," I told the other contestants sheepishly. "My cousin is, er, very **nervous** because of the tension of the competition."

The other chefs didn't buy it. They began to throw cabbage heads and ROTTEN EGGS at me.

Pffffft!

To save myself, I hid inside a garbage can. I reemerged at the end of the day's competition. Unfortunately for me, I was greeted by the flashing cameras of all of the photographers covering the competition. And by then, I SMELLED like a sewer in the hot, sticky month of August. I imagined the headlines of the newspapers the next day: "Geronimo Stilton Stinks!"

"Don't worry!" Trap said. "I'll take care of it!"

Trap pulled me behind the screen.

He SHOVED me into a large pot.

He hosed me down with a bottle of water.

He dried me off with a dishrag.

He combed my fur with a fork.

Finally, he greased my whiskers with olive oil, then he dressed me as a waiter and pushed me out from behind the screen.

"Now, go serve my DiSHeS with class, understand?" he squeaked. "We must win!"

WHEN TRAP IS AROUND, IT'S NEVER GOOD FOR ME!

Ouch! How awful!

① WHEN TRAP MOCKED THE OTHER COOKS, THEY ALL THREW ROTTEN EGGS AT ME, NOT HIM!

② I DIDN'T KNOW WHAT TO DO, SO TO SAVE MYSELF, I HID IN THE TRASH CAN! HOW STINKY!

Blech!

③ WHEN I CAME OUT, I STANK LIKE A SEWER RAT, AND THE PHOTOGRAPHERS TOOK A TON OF PHOTOS!

Are you Geronimo Stilton!?

Poor me!

You stink!

4 TO CLEAN ME UP, TRAP SHOVED ME INTO A POT AND SHOWERED ME WITH BOTTLED WATER.

I'll take care of it!

What are you doing?

It's the final touch!

THEN HE DRIED ME WITH A DISHRAG AND COMBED MY WHISKERS WITH A FORK.

6 FINALLY HE DRESSED ME LIKE A WAITER AND TOLD ME TO SERVE HIS DISHES WITH CLASS!

Huh?

Yum Yum Yum Yum Yum!

For the first time, I got a glimpse of the dishes my cousin had cooked. They looked delicious, and they SMELLED divine! I licked my whiskers.

So Trap *did* know how to cook! Why had he made me taste all of those DISGUSTING dishes, then? How strange!

Voilà!

But I couldn't stop to think about it because my cousin tweaked my tail and began shrieking in my ear.

"Come on, Geronimo, hurry up!" he squeaked.

"The judges are waiting! Don't make me look **BAD**, I beg you. And above all, try to look like a waiter!"

Try to look like a waiter? What did that mean? I shrugged and placed a napkin on my left arm, trying my best. Then I stepped forward **unsteadily**, my shiny, olive oil–coated whiskers **trembling** nervously. **How stressful!**

I tried to balance all of the plates at the same time without stumbling and without **spilling** anything. Creamy cheddar, it was **TOUGH**! I served the judges Trap's food and stood there silently while they **crunched** and **munched**.

The first judge was the famous *Saucy Le Paws*, the biggest pasta expert on Mouse Island.

The second judge was **GORDON RATSEY**,

the most famouse celebrity chef on Mouse Island. He was known for being very, very hard to please. Every time he tasted something, he said, "**UGH!** Not bad, but it needed a little more salt," or "**UGH!** Not bad, but it needed less butter . . ."

He's a pro with pasta, whether it's lasagna, tagliolini, ravioli, or spaghetti!

SAUCY LE PAWS

An award-winning chef who is very intimidating. Everyone is afraid of him because he's very critical and he doesn't like anything!

GORDON RATSEY

The third judge was *Julia Mouselet*, author of the celebrated cookbook *The Delight of Cooking with Cheese*. She was famouse for being a tremendous chatterbox!

The fourth judge was **Rodento McEgo**, a very serious food critic with a waxed

She wrote a famous cookbook called *The Delight of Cooking with Cheese*. She doesn't know how to be quiet!

Julia Mouselet

He's a very famous food critic with a tiny waxed mustache and a very big ego!

Rodento McEgo

mustache. He always wore very **elegant** tails and a top hat.

The four judges tasted all of the contestants' dishes in **silence**. After each tasting, each judge raised a scorecard with a number on it from **1** to **10**. But none of the contestants earned a score above a **6**!

Holey cheese! These judges were very **TOUGH**! When it was finally Trap's turn, Saucy tasted the dishes quietly before he announced his score:

"Very tasty: My vote is eight!"

Gordon Ratsey grumbled, "Ugh! Not bad, but it needed a little more salt. Still, my vote is eight!"

Julia Mouselet consulted her famouse cookbook and shrieked with delight.

"This chef has executed to *perfection* the recipe on page thirty-three of my book," she said proudly. "My vote is eight! And he has nice whiskers, too. They remind me of my cousin's uncle's nephew Fred's. . . ."

She would have **gone on** talking for at least an hour, but Rodento McEgo leaned over and plugged her mouth with a piece of bread.

"My vote is eight!" he announced.

The host of the contest stepped up to the microphone.

"The winner of the **first challenge** is Contestant Chef One-seventeen: Trap Stilton of New Mouse City!" he said. "Congratulations!"

"Yes!" Trap cried out. "I'm the best!"

I'm the best!

PAWS OFF, MISS!

As soon as Trap stopped rejoicing, Julia Mouselet approached the **screen**. Her glasses were studded with rhinestones, and she had a high-pitched, dramatic squeak.

"Now that you've won, Contestant Chef One-seventeen, what's in that TRUNK you have hidden behind this screen?"

She tried to push the screen aside with her paw, but Trap was too quick. He *poked* her paw with a rolling pin.

Paws off!

Ouch!

"Not so fast!" he yelled. "Paws off, miss! Every cook has his SECRETS,

and I have a few of my own. . . ."

Trap quickly closed and **locked** the trunk. Then he put the **key** on a string and hung it around his neck so that no mouse could open the trunk unexpectedly.

How strange!

I was about to ask for an explanation when he began pushing me toward the kitchen.

"Don't try to be sly, Cousin," he said shrewdly. "I did all the cooking, so you *wash the dishes!*"

I stared at the stack of dishes — it was a **mile high**!

I cooked, so you wash!

What?

The dishes were also **gREaSy** and smelled worse than the sewers of New Mouse City. What a **TERRIBLE** job! And while it's true that Trap had done the cooking, I hadn't even gotten to enjoy the **fOOD**!

By the time I had finished washing everything, it was late afternoon. There weren't any more challenges scheduled for the day, so I thought I'd **relax** a bit. I was just about to take a cheddar-scented bubble bath when Trap grabbed me by the ear and dragged me to his camper parked outside.

Once there, he insisted I taste one **disgusting** dish after another. Trap said he was preparing for the next day.

Yuck! Poor me!

While I swallowed each awful mouthful, I wondered how Trap had cooked such delicious dishes during the contest but everything he

had made *me* taste was so terrible. Then I realized it was probably just another one of his PRACTICAL JOKES! Trap loves playing silly little jokes on me.

When he finally let me go, I had such a STOMACHACHE! I had to swallow a **gigantic** antacid to help me digest everything. Then I climbed into bed and tried to get some rest.

I **tossed** and **turned** for hours before I finally fell asleep. In my dreams,

Oh, my poor stomach!

a portrait of Count Ludwig von Cheddar on the castle wall came to *life*! The count did nothing but wail and complain about having a terrible STOMACHACHE. In the morning, I woke from my nightmare covered in sweat. I barely slept a wink!

Oh, poor, poor me!

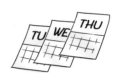

SEVEN CHEFS REMAIN!

For the rest of the WEEK, the large kitchen in the castle was the site of one competition after another.

On Monday the chefs had cooked appetizers.

On Tuesday they made first courses.

On Wednesday roasts were on the menu.

On Thursday it was fish dishes.

Yay!

On Friday they made cheese.

On Saturday it was dessert.

And Sunday would be the final round!

TRAP STILTON

CHEF MOUSARDEE

BETTY BAKERMOUSE

Each round, another chef was **ELIMINATED**. By Saturday evening, all of the **defeated** chefs had left the competition with their tails between their legs.

Only seven chefs remained.

The seven best chefs on Mouse Island.

But at the end, only one would win.

That mouse would receive the Great Golden Fork.

He or she would be Super Chef of the Year!

THE FINAL SEVEN CHEFS

I. SAMMY SUGARPAWS HE'S ONE OF THE FINEST PASTRY CHEFS IN NEW MOUSE CITY.

2. BETTY BAKERMOUSE SHE TRAVELS AS MUCH AS SHE CAN AND SPECIALIZES IN FOOD FROM AROUND THE WORLD.

3. RENÉE BRÛLÉE CALLED "THE SOPHISTICATED CHEF," SHE IS AN EXPERT IN FRENCH HAUTE CUISINE.

4. BLAINE MCVAIN

HIS NICKNAME IS "THE STAR" BECAUSE HE ALWAYS BRAGS ABOUT HIS DISHES. HE SAYS HE DOESN'T SPECIALIZE IN ANYTHING BECAUSE HE'S THE BEST AT EVERYTHING!

5. STELLA SEAWHISKERS

HER NICKNAME IS "THE FISHERMOUSE" BECAUSE SHE IS GREAT AT FISH DISHES.

6. CHARLIE CUSTARD

HIS NICKNAME IS "THE EGG WIZARD" BECAUSE HE SPECIALIZES IN EGG DISHES.

7. TRAP STILTON

THE JOURNALISTS HAVE NICKNAMED HIM "THE MYSTERY CHEF" BECAUSE OF HIS NOW-FAMOUSE SCREEN. NO ONE KNOWS YET WHAT HIS SPECIALTIES ARE! HIS ASSISTANT AND TASTER IS GERONIMO STILTON.

The **winning** chef would get to appear on the hit television show MouseChef! And the winning chef would become famouse all over Mouse Island.

As we watched the ELIMINATED contestants head home, Trap chuckled under his breath. "See you later!" he said.

I, on the other paw, felt **SORRY** for the chefs who had to leave. They had been up against tough competition, and I didn't like to see them go.

See you later!

On Saturday **night**, the remaining chefs went to their rooms early.

Some reviewed recipes, some **shined** their pots and pans, and some went to bed **early** so they would be fresh and

66

rested for the next day.

Sunday would be the day of the **FINAL** round in the **Super Chef Contest**. Every contestant would have to show the judges his or her finest work. It wouldn't be easy to win the **Great Golden Fork**!

All of the chefs were very nervous that night. I offered to make everyone chamomile tea. I'm a modest mouse, but I must admit that I make a *delicious* and **relaxing** cup of tea! Still, the only chef who seemed calm that night was my cousin Trap. He hummed and whistled happily while everyone else trembled with nerves!

Cheers!

"Tra-la-la!" sang Trap. "The winner is here!"

How strange! Why

was Trap so sure of himself when the other chefs were all so **nervous**?

When I offered my cousin a nice cup of chamomile tea, he brushed me aside.

"You drink it, Cuz!" he squeaked. "I don't need to. I'm already **SOOOOOOO** relaxed, because I'm sure I'll **WIN**!

Then he dragged his mega-trunk on wheels behind his screen. A moment later, I heard again a familiar **buzzing** sound. And then Trap began to snore, as usual.

ZZZZZZZZZZZZZZZZZ!

The chamomile tea I had made should have made me very **sleepy**, but I was wide **awake**. Even though I wasn't competing, I was just as anxious as the other chefs about the next day's contest!

I was sitting up in bed reading to pass the time until I was tired enough to sleep when

a **TERRIBLE** storm struck the countryside outside my window. The summer sky lit up with flashes of lightning as thunder shook the entire *castle*!

A moment later, all the lights went out. **SQUEAK!**

FOR THE LOVE OF CHEESE...

I was finally able to **FALL ASLEEP** many hours later when the thunder and lightning had stopped and the silence returned.

I woke up the next morning when my cousin's cell phone rang. It was my aunt Sweetfur calling. She has the loudest squeak ever, so I could hear the entire conversation clearly.

"So, dear, how was the party you had for your friends?" she asked Trap. "Did they like the dishes I prepared? Was the Gorgonzola soufflé good? And how about the three-cheese lasagna?"

Soufflé? Lasagna? Huh?

Was the soufflé good?

What was going on?

"And tell me how the **fondue** with croutons turned out," Aunt Sweetfur continued. "Was it melted enough? And was the eggplant Parmesan **COOKED** enough? And how was the ricotta pie? And the roast? And the cheesecake? And everything else?"

For the love of cheese, I couldn't believe my ears! Those were the dishes Trap had cooked during the competition!

"Thanks again, Aunt Sweetfur!" Trap replied into the phone. "Everything was **delicious**! My friends devoured it all! You're the **BEST** cook in New Mouse City. Bye!"

What a scam! It sounded like Trap had cheated!

Thanks again! It was delicious!

Hmmm...

Done!

Hee, hee, hee!

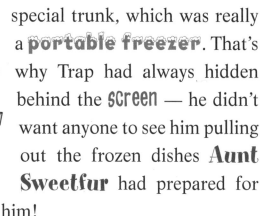

But how had he done it?

Aunt Sweetfur had cooked all the dishes, but how had Trap kept them fresh? Hmmm . . . of course! He had put them in his special trunk, which was really a portable freezer. That's why Trap had always hidden behind the screen — he didn't want anyone to see him pulling out the frozen dishes **Aunt Sweetfur** had prepared for him!

The plug I had seen on the night we arrived was for the freezer! And the strange buzzing noise . . .

yup, it had been the **freezer**!

So that's why everything my cousin cooked **tasted** horrible but he still won all of the competitions. During the contests, he DEFROSTED Aunt Sweetfur's delicious dishes, while his practice dishes were what he had really made (and they were truly **disgusting**, believe me!).

ZZZZZZZZ!

By now, it was very clear to me: My cousin Trap had **CHEATED**!

I leaped out of bed and pushed Trap's *SCREEN* aside.

"I can't believe it, **Trap**!" I

Hee, hee, hee!

squeaked. "**You cheated!** You tricked everyone. Shame on you! It's time for you to **confess**!"

Trap didn't look ashamed at all, though.

"But don't you think I'm a **GENIUS**, Cousin?" Trap replied. "I should win the contest just for my cleverness."

I shook my head in **disbelief**. But before I could say anything, he threw open the freezer.

"This is the secret to how I'll win the title **Super Chef of the Year**!" he exclaimed. "Look at this beautiful food! Smell the **amazing** aroma!"

I looked, but the only thing I saw in the freezer was an **OOZING** glob of green slime! And I smelled it, too: Pee-yoo! What a stench!

It smelled like rotten eggs, moldy socks, and Gorgonzola with worms — **combined**! **BLECH!**

The thunderstorm the previous night had caused the castle to lose **electrical** power, and the **freezer** had been shut off, too! That meant all of the food had gone bad . . . and now it was covered in a swarm of flies!

OUCH! I DISLOCATED MY KNEE!

Trap gasped in horror.

"Noooo!" he squeaked as his snout turned pale "What a **disaster**! This is a complete cat-astrophe! It's a **TRAGEDY**!"

He *dove* toward the fridge in an attempt to save some of the food, but he slipped in the oozing *green* slime. 1

Then he did a **flip** with a twist,

Oooooops!

Help!

shouted "Help!", and crash-landed on the ground, bashing his knee! **BANG!** 2

A second later, he started to yell and squeak in pain: "Ouch! Ouchie! Ow, ow, ow! I think I DISLOCATED my kneecap. I broke my knee! I sprained my paw! I'm in big trouble!" 3

And then he fainted. 4

I quickly REVIVED him and then hurried to the door of the room, where I called for help. It turned out there was a DOCTOR staying at the castle.

Ow, ow, ow!

3

4

The doctor took one look at Trap and confirmed that my cousin really had DISLOCATED his kneecap, BROKEN his other knee, and sprained his paw!

I called an ambulance, and Trap had to be taken out of the castle on a STRETCHER.

As he left, some of the other chefs kindly wished him a quick recovery, but others grinned, rubbing their paws together.

How do you feel?

Good luck!

Poor guy

"Excellent! Very good!" one chef muttered.

"That's one less chef to defeat!" another mumbled.

"This will make it easier to **WIN**!" a third chef added.

Julia Mouselet approached the stretcher.

"Are you **WITHDRAWING** from the competition, Trap?" she asked.

Trap almost leaped off the stretcher

"No!" he squeaked. "I will not withdraw! I nominate *Geronimo* as my replacement!"

But many of the chefs PROTESTED:

Are you withdrawing from the competition?

Excellent!

"Oh no! That's not fair! Trap is the chef who entered the contest! If he goes, he is disqualified!"

A contest official frantically consulted the contest's large rule book.

"Ladies and gentlemice, the rules are very clear," he explained. "Article Seven-thirty-seven says: If a contestant is forced to drop out of the contest for any reason, he or she can nominate his or her assistant as a replacement chef."

"*No, no, no!*" I squeaked. "I couldn't possibly accept."

I had had enough of tasting and cooking and scrubbing pots and pans, and above all else, of my cousin's CHEATING!

"So you're ABANDONING me in my moment of need?" Trap accused me from his stretcher. "Here I am with a dislocated knee, and you're thinking only of yourself. I didn't think you were so selfish, Cousin!"

"But I've been helping you all week!" I protested. "I was your victim, your taster, your assistant, and even your DISHWASHER! Now I would like to go home. I have so much work to do at the office, and . . ."

I trailed off. Trap was blowing his nose on my TIE, sobbing like a tiny mouselet.

Everyone around us was watching and shaking their heads.

"What a heartless rodent!" someone muttered.

"How could he abandon a relative like that?"

At that point, I **gave in**.

"Oh, all right!" I agreed. "I will compete in your place, Trap! But no more cheating! I'll compete fairly. Do you understand?"

He put his chef's hat on my head.

"Take this," he squeaked, "and compete as you wish. Just whatever you do, **WIN!** I want the Great Golden Fork. Work hard, and don't make me look bad!"

Moldy mozzarella! How stressful. Would I be able to do it?

SOMETHING SPECIAL — NO, AMAZING!

The **first thing** I had to do was decide on the menu. What could I prepare for the final contest that night? It had to be something SiMPLe but **delicious**, traditional but original, filling but light. In other words, it had to be something special — no, something **AMAZING**!

An amazing menu!

But ALAS, nothing came to mind. I'm not bad in the kitchen, but I'm not great, either. I like to cook modest **dishes** to share with friends, but nothing more. In other words, I'm a **NORMAL** cook. I'm nothing exceptional, and I am definitely not a **SuPeR CHef**! How could I possibly win the contest?

Then suddenly, I had an **idea**! I would make something simple, light, and above all, **GENUINE**. It would be something I could prepare by myself without asking for help from anyone. I wanted to win, but I wanted to do it the right way — on my own!

I decided to cook my favorite two dishes: my *Mousetastic Zucchini Pizza* and my *Fabumouse Fruit Salad with Cream*.

I took off my chef's uniform, grabbed my shopping bag, and set out toward the town of Gourmetville, where I remembered seeing tons of **INCREDIBLE** grocery stores. I was sure I would find all of the ingredients I needed to prepare my dishes.

But when I arrived in town, I was astonished. The town was **DESERTED**. All of the stores were **CLOSED** — every last one!

What a disaster!

Now where would I find the ingredients I needed? I headed back toward the CASTLE, feeling very discouraged.

I wanted to win for my cousin and for myself, but it was **impossible** now.

What was I going to do?

Then suddenly, I looked up and realized there was a **farm** in front of me. I had passed by it on my way to Gourmetville, but in my rush, I hadn't noticed it.

There was a sign at the entrance that read:

AUNT MOUSIE'S
FARM
GENUINE ORGANIC
PRODUCE FOR SALE!
EXCELLENT PRICES!

A friendly-looking mouse with **rosy** cheeks stood near the gate. She was wearing an apron with flowers on it and a large **straw** hat.

She smiled at me.

Now what? What a disaster!

GOURMETVILLE

"You look like a mouse with a **PRObLeM**," she said kindly. "Is it a **BIG** problem or a **little** one?"

"Oh!" I squeaked, surprised. "Good day, ma'am! It's true — I have a problem, and it's an **ENORMOUSE** one! You see, I am

competing in the **Super Chef Contest**, but all the stores in Gourmetville are closed and I can't get the ***ingredients*** for my dishes!"

"Of course the stores are **CLOSED**!" she replied with a laugh. "It's the final day of the **Super Chef Contest**. In Gourmetville, that's a city holiday. Everyone takes the day off. But maybe I can **HELP**."

Then she pinched my fur affectionately. Wow, did it **hurt**!

Ouch!

Of course the stores are closed!

"Thank you kindly, ma'am," I replied, **rubbing** my cheek. "But I don't know how you could help me."

"We'll see about that!" she squeaked. Then she reached out and grabbed my shopping list. "Give me the list! I'll figure out how to help you **WIN** the contest!"

OPERATION MOUSETASTIC PIZZA

Aunt Mousie grasped me by the paw and pulled me onto the farm.

"Come on," she squeaked. "We have work to do!"

First she brought me to the VEGETABLE GARDEN. Then she grabbed a wicker

Cherry tomatoes . . .

basil . . .

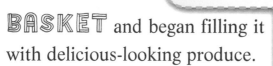

BASKET and began filling it with delicious-looking produce.

She dashed back and forth from one end of the farm to another, putting more and more into the basket. There were ripe *cherry tomatoes*, bunches of fragrant fresh basil, three beautiful PEPPERS, two small zucchinis, and some seasonal FRESH FRUIT she picked straight from the tree!

. . . and peppers!

And fresh fruit!

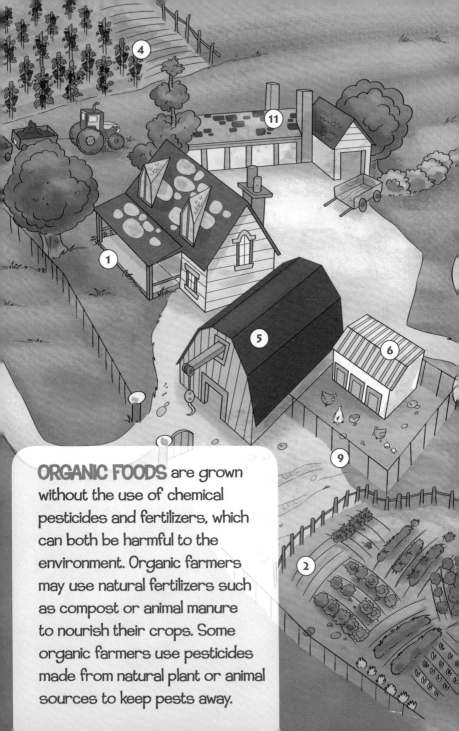

ORGANIC FOODS are grown without the use of chemical pesticides and fertilizers, which can both be harmful to the environment. Organic farmers may use natural fertilizers such as compost or animal manure to nourish their crops. Some organic farmers use pesticides made from natural plant or animal sources to keep pests away.

Next, Aunt Mousie brought me to the **barn**. She introduced me to her favorite cow, Margherita. Then Aunt Mousie told me to fill a pail with milk — directly from the cow!

Unfortunately, I am not very experienced when it comes to milking cows. To protest, first Margherita **squirted** me in the eye with milk. Next, she **STOMPED** on my paw. And finally, she *kicked* me in the tail.

OUCH! I didn't realize farm life could be so hard!

But something worse was still to come . . .

Next Aunt Mousie pushed me into the chicken coop and ordered me to fetch some **eggs**.

"You must be gentle with my chickadees, understand?" she explained. "Otherwise they will get **very angry**!"

I was gentle as, well, a MOUSE (I even said please!). But the hens still pecked my entire body with their sharp little beaks! **MOLDY MOZZARELLA!** Those chickens had terrible tempers!

Then Aunt Mousie pulled me into the pantry. She measured out a pound of flour and passed me a packet of natural yeast.

"Here you go!" she squeaked proudly. "It's

all natural. You'll taste the **GOODNESS**!"

As we **filled** the wicker basket, Aunt Mousie checked off the ingredients on my list.

"Got it, got it, got it!" she mumbled. Suddenly, she GASPED.

"Oh, no!" she squeaked. "We're missing the most important thing for your pizza — the mozzarella!"

She grabbed a bucket and began to beat on it with a ladle, making a **tremendous** racket.

DING! DING! DING!

DING! DING! DING!

"MOZZARELLA EMERGENCY!"

she squeaked at the top of her lungs.

Two rodents in white shirts came running.

Then they led me to the farm's **DAIRY BUILDING**, which is where they made the most delicious cheese.

Yum . . . cheese!

Like all mice, I like cheese. I like fresh cheese, **aged** cheese, extremely aged cheese, stinky cheese, and **incredibly stinky** cheese. In other words, I like it all! I just love cheese! But my *favorite* cheese of all is mozzarella. And there, right in front of my eyes, the two rodents made me the most enormouse piece of fresh, delicious mozzarella!

YUM! I felt like the luckiest mouse in the WORLD.

GO WIN FOR ME!

A short while later, I had **everything** I needed. It ended up being so much that the wicker basket wasn't big enough. I had to **LOAD** everything into a wheelbarrow!

I thanked Aunt Mousie with all my **heart**.

"Thank you so much!" I told her. "How can I ever repay you?"

"Don't **WORRY** about it," she squeaked, kissing me on the cheek. "Just win the

Smooch!

Thanks for everything!

contest! And when you do, be sure to tell everyone that you got your ingredients from **Aunt Mousie's Farm**!"

"Thank you!" I replied. "But I'm not sure I'll win. The other chefs are very good . . . "

"Don't worry, you will win!" she WHiSPeReD in my ear. "The secret to **good cooking** is in the quality of the ingredients! And I grow nothing but the best on my farm! **Go win for me!**"

Go win for me!

Heeeeelp!

Then she gave me a big push, and the wheelbarrow and I began rolling down a very steep hill.

"Heeeeeelp!" I squeaked.

Somehow, I managed to hang on to the wheelbarrow. I made it back to the castle just in the nick of time. The final round of the Super Chef Contest was about to begin! Just as I approached the castle, the wheelbarrow HIT a rock and flew skyward, making a

Heeeeeelp!

perfect arc through the air. I was gripping the wheelbarrow so **TIGHTLY** that I went along with it!

The wheelbarrow and I passed through an open window and landed **right** in the castle's kitchen, **right** in the place assigned to me, **right** at the moment the head judge announced the beginning of the contest!

I had made

Squeak!

it by a WHISKER! I started cooking right away, putting all of my energy into my dishes. I wanted to **WIN**, but not for myself. I wanted to win for Aunt Sweetfur, who had made Trap's delicious dishes. And for Aunt Mousie, who had been so GENEROUS!

So I prepared the most incredible Mousetastic Zucchini Pizza I could, followed by the most Fabumouse Fruit Salad with Cream I had ever whipped up!

I knew I had done my very **best**, but when it was my turn to stand before the judges, my heart was in my throat. My whiskers trembled anxiously, and my knees were knocking from the tension.

One at a time the judges tasted my dishes.
One at a time they closed their eyes.
One at a time they licked their lips.
But no one said a word.

Then they began *whispering* among themselves.

The tension was almost too much to bear!

Finally, the judges all **scribbled** on slips of paper that they handed to the host of the competition.

"Hmmm," he mumbled solemnly. "The winner of this year's contest is Contestant Chef Number One-seventeen, Trap Stilton. I mean, it's his assistant and replacement chef — *Geronimo Stilton*!"

After a slight pause, he continued. "Contestant Chef One-seventeen's menu

How stressful!

Hmmm . . .

Hmmm . . .

Hmmm . . .

Hmmm . . .

was the **simplest**, but also the **tastiest** and the **HEALTHIEST**. The judges could tell it was prepared with genuine, fresh ingredients. congratulations!"

I was so shocked and relieved that I fainted!

I came to a moment later when Rodento McEgo poured a ladle of **icy cold** water over my head.

"Wake up!" he squeaked at me. "You won, and now we have to give you the **prize!**"

A moment later, I received the famous **Great Golden Fork**. Luckily for me, my chef's hat disguised the **ENORMOUSE** bump on my head!

Wake up!

Huh?

As soon as I accepted the prize, my cousin Trap arrived, using a crutch to **hobble** over to me, his leg in a plaster cast.

He tweaked my ear affectionately.

"Nicely done, Geronimo," he said. "You were very good, but I'm afraid I am the **HEAD CHEF**, so . . . I'll keep the **Great Golden Fork**!"

Then he snatched the prize right out of my paw! I **sighed** and let him take it. I had

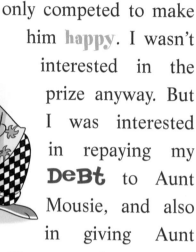

The Great Fork is mine!

only competed to make him happy. I wasn't interested in the prize anyway. But I was interested in repaying my DeBt to Aunt Mousie, and also in giving Aunt Sweetfur credit. They were the reason is Trap and I had won, and I had to be sure everyone knew it.

So when the television crew from **MOUSECHEF** began filming a moment later, I was ready.

"Dear rodent friends, I want to reveal a secret," I said, looking straight at the camera. "EVERYTHING Trap cooked was made by Aunt Sweetfur. She is the **REAL** head chef of our team. And the reason I won the Super Chef Contest was because of Aunt Mousie of **AUNT MOUSIE'S FARM**! She taught me that in order to cook well, you need healthy, fresh ingredients that are simple and genuine, just like those she produces at her **FARM**!"

After that **MOUSECHEF** broadcast, healthy cooking exploded all over Mouse Island. And back in New Mouse City, every mouse who saw me on TV suddenly wanted to learn the recipe for my Mousetastic Pizza and Fabumouse Fruit Salad!

Who would have thought? Life is full of surprises!

Don't miss any of my other fabumouse adventures!

#1 Lost Treasure of the Emerald Eye — **#2 The Curse of the Cheese Pyramid** — **#3 Cat and Mouse in a Haunted House** — **#4 I'm Too Fond of My Fur!** — **#5 Four Mice Deep in the Jungle**

#6 Paws Off, Cheddarface! — **#7 Red Pizzas for a Blue Count** — **#8 Attack of the Bandit Cats** — **#9 A Fabumouse Vacation for Geronimo** — **#10 All Because of a Cup of Coffee**

#11 It's Halloween, You 'Fraidy Mouse! — **#12 Merry Christmas, Geronimo!** — **#13 The Phantom of the Subway** — **#14 The Temple of the Ruby of Fire** — **#15 The Mona Mousa Code**

#16 A Cheese-Colored Camper — **#17 Watch Your Whiskers, Stilton!** — **#18 Shipwreck on the Pirate Islands** — **#19 My Name Is Stilton, Geronimo Stilton** — **#20 Surf's Up, Geronimo!**

#21 The Wild, Wild West

#22 The Secret of Cacklefur Castle

A Christmas Tale

#23 Valentine's Day Disaster

#24 Field Trip to Niagara Falls

#25 The Search for Sunken Treasure

#26 The Mummy with No Name

#27 The Christmas Toy Factory

#28 Wedding Crasher

#29 Down and Out Down Under

#30 The Mouse Island Marathon

#31 The Mysterious Cheese Thief

Christmas Catastrophe

#32 Valley of the Giant Skeletons

#33 Geronimo and the Gold Medal Mystery

#34 Geronimo Stilton, Secret Agent

#35 A Very Merry Christmas

#36 Geronimo's Valentine

#37 The Race Across America

#38 A Fabumouse School Adventure

#39 Singing Sensation

#40 The Karate Mouse

#41 Mighty Mount Kilimanjaro

#42 The Peculiar Pumpkin Thief

#43 I'm Not a Supermouse!

#44 The Giant
Diamond Robbery

#45 Save the White
Whale!

#46 The Haunted
Castle

#47 Run for the Hills,
Geronimo!

#48 The Mystery in
Venice

#49 The Way of
the Samurai

#50 This Hotel Is
Haunted!

#51 The Enormouse
Pearl Heist

#52 Mouse in Space!

#53 Rumble in
the Jungle

#54 Get into Gear,
Stilton!

#55 The Golden
Statue Plot

#56 Flight of the
Red Bandit

Special Edition!

The Hunt for the
Golden Book

#57 The Stinky
Cheese Vacation

#58 The Super
Chef Contest

#59 Welcome to
Moldy Manor

*Don't miss
my journey
through time!*

Check out these exciting Thea Sisters adventures!

Thea Stilton and the Dragon's Code

Thea Stilton and the Mountain of Fire

Thea Stilton and the Ghost of the Shipwreck

Thea Stilton and the Secret City

Thea Stilton and the Mystery in Paris

Thea Stilton and the Cherry Blossom Adventure

Thea Stilton and the Star Castaways

Thea Stilton: Big Trouble in the Big Apple

Thea Stilton and the Ice Treasure

Thea Stilton and the Secret of the Old Castle

Thea Stilton and the Blue Scarab Hunt

Thea Stilton and the Prince's Emerald

Thea Stilton and the Mystery on the Orient Express

Thea Stilton and the Dancing Shadows

Thea Stilton and the Legend of the Fire Flowers

Thea Stilton and the Spanish Dance Mission

Thea Stilton and the Journey to the Lion's Den

Thea Stilton and the Great Tulip Heist

Thea Stilton and the Chocolate Sabotage

Thea Stilton and the Missing Myth

Be sure to read all of our magical special edition adventures!

THE KINGDOM OF FANTASY

THE QUEST FOR PARADISE:
THE RETURN TO THE KINGDOM OF FANTASY

THE AMAZING VOYAGE:
THE THIRD ADVENTURE IN THE KINGDOM OF FANTASY

THE DRAGON PROPHECY:
THE FOURTH ADVENTURE IN THE KINGDOM OF FANTASY

THE VOLCANO OF FIRE:
THE FIFTH ADVENTURE IN THE KINGDOM OF FANTASY

THE SEARCH FOR TREASURE:
THE SIXTH ADVENTURE IN THE KINGDOM OF FANTASY

THEA STILTON: THE JOURNEY TO ATLANTIS

THEA STILTON: THE SECRET OF THE FAIRIES

THEA STILTON: THE SECRET OF THE SNOW

MEET GERONIMO STILTONiX

He is a spacemouse — the Geronimo Stilton of a parallel universe! He is captain of the spaceship *MouseStar 1*. While flying through the cosmos, he visits distant planets and meets crazy aliens. His adventures are out of this world!

#1 Alien Escape

#2 You're Mine, Captain!

#3 Ice Planet Adventure

Meet
GERONIMO STILTONOOT

He is a cavemouse—Geronimo Stilton's ancient ancestor! He runs the stone newspaper in the prehistoric village of Old Mouse City. From dealing with dinosaurs to dodging meteorites, his life in the Stone Age is full of adventure!

#1 The Stone of Fire

#2 Watch Your Tail!

#3 Help, I'm in Hot Lava!

#4 The Fast and the Frozen

#5 The Great Mouse Race

#6 Don't Wake the Dinosaur!

#7 I'm a Scaredy-Mouse!

Meet
CREEPELLA VON CACKLEFUR

I, *Geronimo Stilton*, have a lot of mouse friends, but none as **spooky** as my friend CREEPELLA VON CACKLEFUR! She is an enchanting and MYSTERIOUS mouse with a pet bat named **Bitewing**. YIKES! I'm a real 'fraidy mouse, but even I think CREEPELLA and her family are AWFULLY fascinating. I can't wait for you to read all about CREEPELLA in these fa-mouse-ly funny and **spectacularly spooky** tales!

#1 The Thirteen Ghosts

#2 Meet Me in Horrorwood

#3 Ghost Pirate Treasure

#4 Return of the Vampire

#5 Fright Night

#6 Ride for Your Life!

ABOUT THE AUTHOR

 Born in New Mouse City, Mouse Island, **GERONIMO STILTON** is Rattus Emeritus of Mousomorphic Literature and of Neo-Ratonic Comparative Philosophy. For the past twenty years, he has been running *The Rodent's Gazette*, New Mouse City's most widely read daily newspaper.

Stilton was awarded the Ratitzer Prize for his scoops on *The Curse of the Cheese Pyramid* and *The Search for Sunken Treasure*. He has also received the Andersen 2000 Prize for Personality of the Year. One of his bestsellers won the 2002 eBook Award for world's best ratlings' electronic book. His works have been published all over the globe.

In his spare time, Mr. Stilton collects antique cheese rinds and plays golf. But what he most enjoys is telling stories to his nephew Benjamin.

1. Main entrance
2. Printing presses (where the books and newspaper are printed)
3. Accounts department
4. Editorial room (where the editors, illustrators, and designers work)
5. Geronimo Stilton's office
6. Helicopter landing pad

THE RODENT'S GAZETTE

Map of New Mouse City

Map of Mouse Island

1. Big Ice Lake
2. Frozen Fur Peak
3. Slipperyslopes Glacier
4. Coldcreeps Peak
5. Ratzikistan
6. Transratania
7. Mount Vamp
8. Roastedrat Volcano
9. Brimstone Lake
10. Poopedcat Pass
11. Stinko Peak
12. Dark Forest
13. Vain Vampires Valley
14. Goose Bumps Gorge
15. The Shadow Line Pass
16. Penny Pincher Castle
17. Nature Reserve Park
18. Las Ratayas Marinas
19. Fossil Forest
20. Lake Lake
21. Lake Lakelake
22. Lake Lakelakelake
23. Cheddar Crag
24. Cannycat Castle
25. Valley of the Giant Sequoia
26. Cheddar Springs
27. Sulfurous Swamp
28. Old Reliable Geyser
29. Vole Vale
30. Ravingrat Ravine
31. Gnat Marshes
32. Munster Highlands
33. Mousehara Desert
34. Oasis of the Sweaty Camel
35. Cabbagehead Hill
36. Rattytrap Jungle
37. Rio Mosquito

Dear mouse friends,
Thanks for reading, and farewell
till the next book.
It'll be another whisker-licking-good
adventure, and that's a promise!

Geronimo Stilton